Ellie Ultra is published by Stone Arch Books,
A Capstone Imprint
1710 Roe Crest Drive
North Mankato, Minnesota 56003
www.mycapstone.com

For Milla, a super leader — love, Mom

Library of Congress Cataloging-in-Publication Data is
available on the Library of Congress website.

ISBN: 978-1-4965-5239-6 (hardcover) — 978-1-4965-5241-9
(paperback) — 978-1-4965-5243-3 (ebook PDF)

Summary: It's time to vote for class president at
Winkopolis Elementary School. But Ellie isn't a shoe-in
for the role when her archnemesis, Dex Diggs, decides
to run too.

Editor: Alison Deering
Designer: Lori Bye

Printed in the United States of America.
010762S18

Superhero for President

written by Gina Bellisario

illustrated by Jessika von Innerebner

STONE ARCH BOOKS
a capstone imprint

TABLE OF CONTENTS

CHAPTER 1

A Good Leader

It was just another day in the city of Winkopolis. Bunnies hopped. Drivers stopped. Shoppers shopped. Everyone was doing the same old ordinary things. Everyone, mind you, but the girl who lived at 8 Louise Lane.

That girl was Ellie Ultra. At Winkopolis Elementary School, she was busy helping her classmate Owen solve a math problem. She multiplied and added speedier than a sailfish with superpowered fins. It was *extra*ordinary.

"The problem is seventeen times two," Ellie told Owen. "First, take seven times two, then carry the one and — *POW!* The answer is thirty-four."

Ellie's brainpower usually helped her outsmart evil aliens. But when the world didn't need Ellie Ultra — third-grade superhero and all-around good kid — her smarts came in handy for tackling two-digit multiplication.

"Oh, I get it now," Owen said. He had been stuck on the same problem for ten minutes. Until Ellie unstuck him, that is. "Thanks for your help."

"Time for social studies," Miss Little said, ringing the class wind chime. "Yesterday, we learned about our country's presidents and the good things they did. Who would like to give an example?"

Payton waved her hand around. "George Washington was honest. He worked with people, even when he didn't agree with them."

"Abraham Lincoln helped everyone be free," Joshua added.

"Right," Miss Little replied. "Being honest. Working together. Helping others. That's what good leaders do."

"They also save the day," Ellie said. "You know, in case an Egyptian pharaoh comes back from the dead with an army of undead mummies. That happened last week!"

Miss Little smiled. Ellie's superhero stories would've surprised most teachers. But Miss Little already knew all about super-villains, thanks to Ellie.

"That's correct," the teacher replied. She closed her textbook. "I think every class needs a good leader. That's why next Friday, we'll be having an election. You will all get to vote for a class president!"

Everyone gasped and clapped.

"Voting is a right that citizens receive, but it's also an honor," Miss Little continued. "As citizens of our class, you'll get the honor of choosing who will lead Room #128. All we need are volunteers who will run for president."

Ellie sat up in her seat. She would make a great class president! She would stand for truth, justice, and more story time.

"I'll volunteer!" she said. "I promise to be a super leader! I'll fight against vampire vegetables and super-villain takeovers. I'll even empty the class recycling bin."

"It looks like we have our first candidate," Miss Little said. "Is anyone else interested in running?" Her eyes skimmed over the room.

In the corner, a hand shot up like an arrow. It belonged to none other than Ellie's archenemy, Dex "Rotten Pineapple Face" Diggs.

"I am," Dex announced. "And when I win, I'm going to rule the whole school. I'll even have a throne — the same one I had at my Bounce X-Treme birthday party. *Bwwa-ha-ha-HA!*" Throwing his head back, he laughed wickedly.

Ellie frowned. Dex was an ordinary kid, but he acted an awful lot like an evil mastermind. He loved to take over stuff, including the twisty slide at recess. Now he was after the school!

Not if I can help it, Ellie thought.

"Being a good leader isn't only about telling people what to do," Miss Little reminded Dex. "It's also about doing good deeds for others."

The teacher took a step back as she spoke, but when she did, she slipped on Dex's markers.

He had a bad habit of leaving them scattered on the floor.

"Oh, dear!" Miss Little cried, stumbling toward the recycling bin. She was going to fall in!

Ellie needed to save her teacher from eco-friendly doom. "I'm coming, Miss Little!" she shouted.

Roaring out of her seat, Ellie zoomed around Miss Little's desk and grabbed the teacher's chair. In the blink of an eye, she swapped the bin and the chair.

Miss Little landed comfortably on the cushion. Ellie zipped back to her own seat.

"Whew! My hero," Miss Little said. She straightened up and smoothed her hair. "Now, Ellie and Dex, you two will have the rest of this week and next to campaign. On Monday next week, you'll each give a speech explaining why you would be a good leader. Then on Friday our class citizens will vote."

As the teacher carried on, Ellie drifted off into a presidential daydream. She imagined herself as the leader of Miss Little's class. She would be fair. Honest. Hardworking. Someone who fought for more field trips and less homework. Someone who stopped bullies. She would ask for extra time on tests for one and all and share her carrots at lunch.

Ellie's daydream lasted until — *briiing!* — the bell rang. She jumped up to put on her cape for her flight home when a shadow moved over her.

"Hey, Super Blooper," said a sinister voice.

With a sigh, Ellie faced the troublemaker. "What do you want, Dex?" she asked.

"I'm here to offer you advice," Dex replied. "Give up now. I'm going to win the election."

Ellie's eyes narrowed. "Why do you think that?"

"It's simple, really. I have a plan that will help me get every last vote. And the best part is, no one can stop me — not even you and your cape. *Bwwa-ha-ha-HA!*" Dex laughed his evil laugh one final time and ran out the door.

Ellie glared. Even with Dex gone, her supersonic hearing picked up his snickering in the hallway. As she listened, her ears burned. The heat traveled down her arms and made her hands glow red-hot.

"I'll show Dex," Ellie said to herself. "I'll prove I'd make a better leader and beat him for good!"

CHAPTER 2

Pizza and Pinball Machines

The next day, the race for class president began.

Ellie hit the ground running. She finished lunch early and made campaign stickers with her best friend, Hannah. Ellie colored the stickers a cheerful purple. Hannah wrote: *Vote for a Hero and Super Kid for President.*

Peel. Stick. Peel. Stick. They stuck the stickers around school, then hurried to Miss Little's room. There, Payton and Amanda were decorating Ellie's campaign posters.

"What do you think, Ellie?" Payton asked.

She held up a poster that read *Flex Your Power: Vote for Ellie!* There was also a picture of Ellie lifting Winkopolis Elementary School high above her head.

Ellie smiled weakly. With her mighty muscles, she had lifted things like baby hippos and uprooted trees. But a school? No way!

"Wow, I look strong. Even for a superhero!" she replied.

"Wait until you hear what I wrote for you!" Amanda flipped her journal open. "It's a special poem for your campaign.

Hip, hip, hooray!

Ellie saves the day!

She's full of honesty, trust, and hope.

Vote for her today!"

"That's a great poem! Thanks!" Ellie replied as Hannah and Payton clapped. "And thanks everyone for your help. Between doing chores and stopping brain-hungry zombies, there's no way I'd be able to make all these stickers and posters by myself!"

"Glad to help!" Hannah said. "Besides, who volunteers to be my study buddy? Ellie!"

"And who cheers for me at my soccer games?" Payton said. "Ellie!"

"And who listens to all my poems?" Amanda said. "Ellie!"

"Ellie! Ellie! Ellie!" the girls chanted. They skipped out to hang the posters in the hall.

Ellie took a deep breath. Her friends knew she would make a good leader. With their support, she could smell victory in the air.

But she could also smell her egg salad from lunch.

"I better throw this away in the cafeteria," Ellie said. She pinched her nose at the stinky leftovers and flew off.

The bell rang just as she returned.

"Future class president, coming through!" Dex hollered. He marched through the doorway carrying a bunch of campaign posters.

Thwack! Thwack! Thwack! Dex slapped them on the wall, one at a time.

Evil Masterminds Rule.

It's Good to Be Bad.

Give Up Now: Vote for Dex.

Ellie shook her head as she read Dex's posters. How could anyone vote for a villain?

Just then Owen popped up with his math workbook. "Ellie, can you show me how to multiply again?" he asked. "Miss Little said there's a math quiz tomorrow. I don't think I'm ready."

"Sure! You can count on me —" Ellie started to say. But before she could finish, Dex butted into the conversation like a bossy ram.

"You know, Owen," he interrupted, "if you vote for me, I'll put an end to math quizzes."

"Really?" Owen replied. He turned away from Ellie. "That would help. A lot."

"I'll also outlaw tests," Dex promised. "No more reading tests, social studies tests, you name it. And I promise to bring an end to the behavior chart." He turned to the chart and glared at a long line of stop sign stickers following his name.

"What else will you do?" Joshua asked. He had overheard everything while he was sharpening his pencil.

"How do all-day recess and a class pinball machine sound?" Dex said. "I'll even add a big-screen TV to the classroom! That way, we can play video games and eat pizza!"

More students gathered around. Soon a crowd had formed. They stared wide-eyed as Dex wooed them with other promises. Only Ellie wasn't wooed. She knew Dex couldn't really give pizza and pinball machines to the class. He was only promising those things to get everyone to vote for him.

So that's his plan, Ellie thought. *Well, he'll see. No one will fall for his promises.*

She started to walk away. But before she got far, strange voices stopped her cold.

"I'll vote for you!"

"Me too!"

"Dex for president!"

The voices belonged to the good citizens of Room #128. They were rooting for the not-so-good guy. Either her classmates had turned into the mastermind's minions, or Ellie had to step up her campaign.

CHAPTER 3

A Winning Recipe

On Saturday, Ellie spent the afternoon rehearsing her speech. "And, as your president, I will help you with your science projects," she said in front of her mirror. "I will fight any experiments that go berserk and stop them from eating the class comfy chair."

"Knock-knock." Mom walked into Ellie's room and handed over a cupcake. "You've been working hard on your speech, so Dad and I thought you deserved a treat. We're rooting for you, Candidate Ultra."

"Thanks, Mom!" Ellie took one bite, and the burst of sweetness sent her brainpower into overdrive. She realized she could bake cupcakes for her fellow class citizens. After all, everyone liked treats with sprinkles!

In no time, Ellie called Hannah over to help with baking.

"We need to make enough for everyone," Ellie said, leading her friend into the kitchen. "It's sure to be a *winning* recipe!"

Hannah measured all the ingredients as Ellie flew up and grabbed a mixing bowl from the top cupboard.

"I heard Owen is voting for Dex," Hannah said, scooping out the flour. "Do you know Dex promised to turn Owen's desk into a rocket ship?"

Ellie nodded. Dex had also promised a class field trip to Mars. Ellie had already seen the red

planet while chasing a runaway asteroid. Personally, she thought the space museum was way more exciting.

After Ellie stirred the batter, Hannah filled the cupcake trays. Baking time!

Ellie took a tray in each hand. Her hands glowed as her heating power cooked the treats until they were plump and golden. Then she set the trays down to cool.

"In gym yesterday, Dex said he'd name the soccer field after Payton," Ellie said. "He's trying to win over my friend! Isn't that funny, Hannah? Hannah?" She turned and noticed Hannah frowning. "What's the trouble? Is a villain on the loose?"

"Not exactly . . ." Hannah replied. "It's just . . . Dex's promise made Payton really happy. She's excited about playing on her own field."

Had Ellie's hearing gone haywire? Payton, her friend and fellow good kid, was going to vote for her true-blue archenemy!

"What about Amanda?" Ellie asked.

Hannah winced. "Dex promised to give her a parrot that can recite her poems. She can't wait. Sorry, Ellie . . ."

Ellie felt her heart sink. Dex had brainwashed her friends! His badness knew no bounds.

"I'm voting for you no matter what Dex promises," Hannah said. "Anyway, I better go. I need to practice for the school play. Auditions for *Dancing Snowflake* are next Monday, and I really want the lead. Will you help me get ready?"

"Of course I'll help," Ellie replied. It was what a good leader would do. But she was starting to wonder if her deeds were good enough to beat Dex.

CHAPTER 4

Wishful Thinking

On Monday at recess, Ellie looked positively presidential. She felt like George Washington with a cape. Smiling brightly, she paraded out to the playground with a tray of cupcakes.

"Treats for Miss Little's class!" she announced.

Classmates ran over and took a cupcake. "Wow, thanks, Ellie!" Payton said.

"Yeah, thanks!" Joshua chimed in.

"Vote for Ellie!" Hannah said at Ellie's side. She was handing out campaign stickers left and right.

Dex swaggered up to the tray. He was wearing a sticker that read *I am your leader*. Ellie's mood immediately soured.

"You made cupcakes, huh?" Dex said, eyeing them suspiciously. "Yuck. They probably have super cooties."

"That doesn't sound very leader-ly," Hannah snapped.

Ellie's hands grew hot. That master meanie had triggered her heating power! She took a breath and tried cooling down.

"How about a cupcake, Dex," she offered politely. "We should support each other for the betterment of our class. Don't you think?"

Dex stood quietly. He was no doubt plotting world domination.

"Nah," he finally answered. "Evil masterminds rule, and superheroes drool." With that, he ran off down the field, laughing all the way.

Ellie lost her cool. Her hands burned more and more until they reached a scorching heat. The cupcake tray melted out of Ellie's fingers, and the sugary goodies tumbled to the ground.

"Oh no!" Hannah cried.

Ellie picked an cupcake off her shoe. "I wonder if this happened to George Washington," she said, wiping away frosting.

Her cupcake idea had flopped. But maybe her speech would go better.

* * *

After a test in social studies, it was time for the candidates to give their speeches. Ellie flew to the front of the class and stood at the podium. She was ready to prove herself, even if it meant getting the stink eye from Dex.

"Go, Ellie!" Hannah cheered as Ellie took her place across from her archenemy.

"Quiet, please," Miss Little said. She turned to the candidates. "Ellie and Dex, one at a time, please explain why you would be a good leader. Ellie, let's start with you."

"As your president, I will be fair," Ellie began. "I will always listen to you, even when we have different opinions. If I make mistakes, I will do my best to fix them." She paused for a moment. "I'll fight mutant pigeons too, in case they invade Winkopolis."

The class clapped. "That was very nice, Ellie," said Miss Little. Then she turned to Dex. "OK, Dex. It's your turn."

"I will begin in the words of Abraham Lincoln, also known as Honest Abe . . ." Dex paused and cleared his throat. "Four score and five minutes ago I brought forth, upon this class, a promise. A promise to turn silent reading into a circus — with acrobats — and get a drinking fountain that squirts ten kinds of fruit juice."

Hannah raised her hand. "How will you do that?" she challenged.

"Let's save our questions until after the speeches are over," Miss Little said to Hannah.

Despite Miss Little's words, Dex answered Hannah with a thin grin.

"I have my ways," he replied. "I can make things happen. Aren't you auditioning for *Dancing Snowflake*?"

Hannah's hand lowered. She nodded a little, looking interested.

"Well, I can give you the lead part in the play," Dex continued. "Imagine. You, the big kahuna, the whole enchilada . . . the *star*."

Hannah's eyes sparkled as Dex went on and on. He even promised to make sure she had new ballet shoes with turbo boosters for extra leaping power!

By the time Dex was finished, Hannah was spellbound.

Ellie couldn't believe it — Dex was winning over her super bestie! "Dex won't stop until he gets every last vote," she said to herself. "But I'll show him. I'll prove I'm the best candidate for the job. And that's a promise!"

* * *

All recess, Ellie had been forced to hand out campaign stickers by herself. Hannah had been busy twirling around the playground, pretending to be the lead in *Dancing Snowflake*.

Ellie dragged her backpack into the kitchen after school and flopped in her seat at the table. *Ruff ruff!* Super Fluffy, Ellie's puppy pal, pawed at her chair. He had been waiting for her to get home to play.

"Not now, Fluffster," Ellie told him. "Dex is taking over the election. I need to figure out how to stop him, or he's going to be President Evil Mastermind!"

Just then a broom popped out of the closet and started sweeping the floor. At the same time, the faucet filled a sink of dirty dishes. A rag set to washing cups and bowls.

Super Fluffy jumped on Ellie's lap as the broom swept past.

"It's magic!" Ellie cried. Maybe it was the work of Hocus Pocus, the most magical villain in Winkopolis. He pulled off all kinds of tricks with one simple word — Alaka*bam!*

Just then Mom swung open the door from the basement laboratory. "Excellent! The kitchen is cleaning itself!" she exclaimed. "That means our newest invention worked — it granted our wish!"

The cleaning chaos wasn't magic, after all — it was *science*! Ellie's parents were genius inventors who made amazing gadgets for a superhero group called B.R.A.I.N. Their creations mostly helped to catch villains, but sometimes they also helped with housework.

"Behold, the Ultra Genie!" Dad appeared with a small gold lamp. "Your wish is the invention's command."

"Wow! Is there a real genie inside?" Ellie asked. She blinked on her X-ray vision and scanned the lamp. She picked up a few bolts and a dust bunny that was shaped like a unicorn. "Yoo-hoo, Genie! Are you in there?"

Dad laughed and shook his head. "The *lamp* grants your wish. It's made out of pennies we found in a wishing well."

"All you have to do is say your wish and rub the lamp," Mom explained. "Then your wish will come true."

The broom swept up some crumbs around their feet, then hopped back into the closet. Ellie glanced at the sink. Clean dishes were now sitting in the drying rack. The faucet had turned itself off.

"The Ultra Genie will be a big help around here," Dad told Ellie. "Just don't use it to ask for more cupcakes, OK?" He put the genie down on the table. "That reminds me . . . how did your speech go? Are you on your way to getting elected, Miss Super President?

"I wish," Ellie said. "The problem is Dex. He's making phony promises, and the class is falling for them! I doubt I'll win, even if I'm the *real* do-gooder."

"When it's time to vote, I'm sure everyone will forget all about Dex's promises," Mom reassured her.

"And they'll remember the good things you've done," added Dad. He turned toward the laboratory door. "Well, we better get back to work. We need to fish some pennies out of the puffer-fish pond. Cyclops tossed them in to wish for baseball cards."

Cyclops was the Ultras' giant, one-eyed iguana. He was always trying a new hobby, like finger-painting and knitting. Now he wanted to start a baseball card collection.

"The Ultra Genie can grant anything," Ellie said as her parents disappeared downstairs. "A clean kitchen . . . baseball cards for Cyclops . . . a rocket ship desk . . . an out-of-this-world field trip . . ."

Suddenly, Alaka*bam!* A magical idea struck. If
Ellie used the genie to grant wishes — things Dex
was only promising — she would win everyone's vote.
And that meant she would win the election!

CHAPTER 5

Poof!

Magic was at Ellie's fingertips as she flew into
school on Wednesday morning. It wasn't Hocus
Pocus' evil hat in her grasp. It was a gadget that
would do good. Good for her class. Good for
Winkopolis. Good for the world.

The Ultra Genie sparkled as Ellie flew past the
library and gym. As she drew closer to Miss Little's

classroom, Ellie's super ears picked up a low hissing sound coming from Payton's locker. *Pfffeet!*

"Drat. My ball!" Payton said, swinging her locker door wide. She picked up a flattened soccer ball.

"What happened?" Ellie asked, floating over. "Did a rhino android step on that? Be careful. One of those beasts can crush a pumpkin with its pinkie toe!"

Payton shook her head. "My soccer spikes put a hole in it. Double drat! It's my lucky ball too! I need it for my game on Saturday. I wish it were fixed."

A wish! Ellie thought. It was the first wish from a class citizen and from Citizen Payton, no less!

"I can help," Ellie offered. Rubbing the Ultra Genie, she said, "I wish Payton's soccer ball would go back to normal."

Poof! Powdery smoke swirled out of the genie's spout. It slowly faded, revealing a good-as-new ball in Payton's hand.

"Whoa!" Payton stared in disbelief. She flipped the ball over, around, and back again. "The hole is gone! That's amazing!"

"It's nothing, really," Ellie said with a giggle. "I can do a whole lot more as class president. So remember to vote for me on Friday!"

"Sure!" Payton hopped away, bouncing her ball from knee to knee.

Just then Joshua trudged up with his skateboard. "I saw that trick you did," he said, a little out of breath. "Can you fix my skateboard? The wheel broke. I was stuck walking all the way to school."

"Your wish is my command!" Ellie said in her best commander-in-chief voice. She gave the genie a rub. "I wish the wheel on Joshua's skateboard were new."

Poof! Smoke escaped the genie and covered the skateboard. Joshua's jaw dropped when the smoke disappeared. His skateboard now had a shiny new wheel.

"Wow!" Joshua said. "Thanks!" He hurried into the room to show everyone.

"Vote for Ellie!" Ellie called after him. She studied the Ultra Genie happily. With it, she could stop a certain third-grade evildoer for sure!

Just then, Dex, the villain himself, popped out of Miss Little's doorway. His pineapple face looked more rotten than usual.

"If it isn't *Sm*ellie Ultra," he said. "I hear you're up to good. When I'm president, I'll put an end to that."

"You're not the only candidate with a plan," Ellie replied coolly. "I have a trick that will help me win. And it will work like magic!"

* * *

Ellie spent the rest of the day granting wishes. She made good on Dex's promise and turned Owen's desk into a rocket ship. She also granted Amanda's wish, giving her friend a squawky-talky parrot. Miss Little looked displeased as the parrot recited Amanda's poems all through language arts.

At recess, Hannah got her wish too.

"I'm the dancing snowflake!" she squealed on the playground. Ellie had granted her the starring role in the school play.

Hannah spun around, the sun glinting off her glittery new costume. She clicked her shoes together, and turbo boosters popped out. *Zoom!* She soared over the soccer field. Payton waved at Hannah from her spot under the scoreboard, which now said *Payton's Field* in bright letters.

At the beginning of social studies, Miss Little rang her chime. "Exciting news, class citizens!

Election Day is on Friday. That's when we will vote for our new president."

"I already know who I'm voting for," Hannah said, adjusting her snowflake hat. "Ellie!"

"I'm voting for Ellie too," Payton added. "Who else would give me a soccer field?"

"And a rocket ship!" said Owen.

"And a parrot!" Amanda said, looking up from her journal. She had been writing a poem about her feathered friend. "My vote is for Ellie!"

"Ellie!" the parrot echoed.

"Ellie! Ellie!" the class chanted.

Miss Little frowned. "A president should do nice things for others," she said. "But remember, being a good leader isn't all about giving gifts."

As everyone quieted down, Ellie sank in her seat. She felt a little bad about granting wishes with the

Ultra Genie. But she'd had to find a way to stop Dex . . .

Joshua stood at the classroom's new fruit-juice drinking fountain. "Ellie, can you add mango juice to this thing?" he asked. "It's my favorite flavor."

"As you wish!" Ellie rubbed the genie. "I wish the fountain made mango juice."

Poof! A mango flavor button appeared on the fountain's control panel. It had more flavors than a fruit-juice factory.

When the smoke cleared, Ellie caught Dex scowling. His plan for class domination was crumbling, but it was probably for the best. After all, what if the evil mastermind became president?

It would be no good, Ellie thought. *No good at all!*

CHAPTER 6

Villain-in-Chief

Election Day! It was the day when ordinary citizens used their extraordinary power — the power to vote.

Ellie made the morning magical. With the Ultra Genie's help, she granted scuba-diving lessons in gym and all-you-can-eat tacos at lunch. In music, she gifted a concert by the famous Winkopolis pop

band, the Bubble Gummers. The class went wild when the band played their biggest hit, "Stuck on You."

Being a genie is fun! Ellie thought as she bounced to the beat.

After the Ultra Genie made apple pie fractions in math, it was time for social studies. Finally the class would flex its voting power!

"I'm voting for you," Hannah said to Ellie, cleaning up one fifth of her pie. "Thanks for giving me the part. It's a wish come true. Your superpowers are the best!"

"Voting is also a superpower," Ellie replied. "How else can you fight for life, liberty, and the pursuit of more story time?"

"I'm picking you too," Payton said from the next row. "My new soccer field is lucky, just like my ball. I scored two goals in the game at recess."

"Hear ye, hear ye!" Miss Little waved slips of paper over her head. "In my hand are ballots. Each of you will receive one ballot to choose a class president. First, our candidates will make a final statement. It's their last chance to win your vote." She called Dex up first.

Dex puffed out his chest and addressed the crowd. "Taking over a classroom isn't easy," he said. "You need the right person for the job. And I'm just the evil mastermind — er, I mean, *candidate* — to do it!" He pounded his fist on the podium in front of him.

Ellie smiled at the Ultra Genie. It was a do-gooding gadget, no doubt. Not only had it won votes for her, but it had also saved her class from having a villain-in-chief.

Just then Owen reached over his rocket ship and tapped Ellie's shoulder. "Look at this," he whispered, holding up his math quiz from last Friday. "I only got one wrong on the quiz. It's because of your help! I'm voting for you since you already make a good leader."

Ellie bit her bottom lip. She had won Owen's vote by simply being helpful. Maybe she didn't need the genie's power, after all.

"Thank you for your, um, speech," Miss Little told Dex as he took a bow. "The class will now hear from Ellie."

Ellie set the Ultra Genie on her desk. As she switched places with Dex, he muttered, "You probably think you'll win. But masterminds always have a plan B — B for *bad*." He stuck out his tongue, then marched to his seat.

At the front of the classroom, Ellie gazed into the crowd. It was full of citizens who were going to pick her for president. Still, she wondered if she could have proved herself without granting their wishes.

But something caught her eye mid-thought. She spotted Dex with the Ultra Genie. That sneak had swiped it off her desk!

Rubbing the genie, Dex announced, "I wish I ruled Winkopolis Elementary School."

Poof! Smoke poured out of the gadget's spout. It swirled over the room like a wild gust of wind, covering books and backpacks, paints and posters.

"Dex! NOOO!" Ellie shouted. If she didn't stop the genie, Dex's wicked wish would come true! Kicking up her fiery feet, she blazed through the smoke as it swallowed the floor, ceiling, and all four walls until . . .

Alaka*bam!* School as Ellie knew it was gone.

CHAPTER 7

Robo-Baddies

A thick, gray fog hung in the air as Ellie stood outside of school. At least, she thought it was school. It looked more like a villain's lair. On each window, someone had taped up signs that read *No Superheroes Allowed!* Remote-controlled monster trucks burned rubber along the ground. They raced from door to door, their headlights searching for super visitors.

Ellie ducked behind a bush, narrowly avoiding their lights. "What is this place?" she whispered to herself.

The school had a playground, but all the equipment was locked up. It also had a teachers' parking lot. But strangely, the lot was empty.

Ellie needed to investigate. When the last monster truck was safely out of sight, she flew across the grounds. A giant inflatable T-Rex loomed over the Winkopolis Elementary School sign, covering the words with its mega mouth. Ellie blinked on her X-ray vision and peered at the sign through the jaws of the great beast.

"Dex Diggs Elementary School," she read out loud. Oh no! The Ultra Genie, her good-wish granting gadget, had granted Dex's way-bad wish!

"Stop superheroes! Stop superheroes!" Suddenly, a group of chanting robots came marching around the far end of the building. They appeared to be ordinary robots, except each bot had a nasty scowl on its face, just like Dex's.

The Dex-bots swung their arms and stomped their feet as they headed toward the main entrance. They walked like the evil mastermind. They talked like the evil mastermind. It could only mean one thing — they were the evil mastermind's minions! But where was the master meanie himself?

Just then the front door of school swung open. "Minions!" a familiar voice called out. "I have a job for you. Come inside. NOW!"

Obediently, the Dex-bots picked up the pace and filed into school. Moments later, Dex emerged with the Ultra Genie. He looked much more menacing. It was as if the genie had turned him into a real honest-to-badness villain.

Peeking out, Dex eyed the school grounds suspiciously. Then he slunk back into the building.

I have to get the Ultra Genie, Ellie thought as the door banged shut. No doubt Dex would use it to wish for more evil stuff. But what? Pet piranhas? A *Not Welcome* mat for his lair?

Whatever it was, Ellie had to stop him. It was time to pay her archenemy a visit.

* * *

The main entrance was the only way into Dex Diggs Elementary School. There, a robot stood guard. It greeted the world with a sourpuss pucker.

Ellie approached carefully. "Excuse me," she said to the bot. "This is my school, and I need to get inside."

At once, bright beams shot out of the minion's eyes. The light swallowed Ellie for a split second before zeroing in on her cape.

"Superhero alert!" the bot announced. Its hands withdrew, and its arms transformed into cannons. The bot aimed them at her.

"Yikes!" Ellie squealed. She sped away as the bot began launching rotten pineapple after rotten pineapple at her. It was a terrible attack of tropical fruit!

Ellie raced across the schoolyard and hid behind a tree. She blinked herself invisible as the bot passed. Once it was safe, she made a break for the entrance. Ellie slipped inside . . . and gasped.

Just like the outside, the school's interior had Dex's evil touch. There were obstacle courses made of broken crayons, crumpled gum wrappers, and past-due library books. Remote-controlled monster trucks roared through, crushing everything under their wheels.

The student gallery, which had been labeled *Oh, the Places I'll Go!*, now read *Oh, the Places I'll Take Over!* Dex had drawn himself on every picture.

There was Dex on top of Mount Everest. Dex on the Great Wall of China. Dex on Mount Rushmore. Dex going over Niagara Falls in a barrel. There was even one of Dex planting a flag on the moon!

Ellie shook her head at the gallery. "If Dex thinks he's going to rule these places, he has lost his mastermind marbles," she said. "Besides, the Moon People already have a president."

Ellie headed for the classrooms, where the kids were learning way-bad lessons. In kindergarten, a robot was teaching the alphabet. There was S for *snotcicle,* T for *toe jam,* and W for *wedgie.* In first and second grade, a robot was demonstrating how to fold a quiz into a hat. The fourth and fifth graders were practicing the stink eye.

Finally Ellie reached Miss Little's room. She was ready to face Dex and take back her parents' invention. But the desk in the corner where Dex normally sat was empty.

"Psst, Ellie! Over here!" Hannah poked her head out from behind a stack of spelling worksheets. There were stacks on every desk. They stretched all the way to the ceiling.

Ellie raced over. "Hannah, this is no time to work on spelling. We need to save the school from Dex!"

"Dex said we can't do anything until we finish our worksheets," Hannah replied. "Guess what he's doing? Eating pizza and playing video games. It's so not fair!"

It was not fair. Not fair at all. "Where is Dex anyway?" Ellie asked.

"I saw him a few minutes ago in the main office. He needed the phone to order pizzas with extra cheese." Hannah looked over Ellie's shoulder at the doorway. "You better go. A robot is coming to drop off more work. You don't want to get stuck with doing long division, believe me." Hannah stretched her fingers, then got back to her worksheet.

Poor class citizens, Ellie thought. They were in a pickle. A jam. A pickle in a jam sandwich. It wasn't a good place to be. *And it's my fault!*

If she hadn't brought the Ultra Genie to school, then Dex couldn't have made his wish. Room #128 would still be the land of the free and the home of the fun projects. And Dex? He would still be a regular bully with an appetite for teasing Ellie!

Suddenly, robots hummed in the distance. The noise was coming from the stairwell and getting closer. Ellie peeked out the door as ten Dex-bots marched past.

"Stop superheroes! Stop superheroes!" the bots chanted. Their arms and legs moved steadily to the beat.

Ellie waited until they were a safe distance away, then headed in the opposite direction. She had only gone a few steps when a bright light struck her.

"Superhero alert! Superhero alert!" Up ahead, another group of Dex-bots stood at the top of the stairs. Their eyebeams locked onto Ellie's cape. She was trapped!

Ellie quickly turned to the first group of bots. "Hey, robo-baddies!" she shouted. "Come and get me! I'm a superhero, see?" She wiggled her cape at them like it was a worm on a hook.

Taking the bait, the troops about-faced and aimed their cannons at Ellie. On the other side of her, the second group did the same thing.

Whump whump! Whump whump! Rotten pineapples fired from both directions.

Ellie flew to the ceiling, letting the fruit pass below her. One after another, the pineapples pummeled the bots. It didn't take long until both groups were completely buried under mushy-brown heaps.

Ellie wiped her hands like her parents did when they solved two problems with one super thought. "That takes care of Dex's robots," she said with a grin.

It hadn't been hard to trick them. They didn't have much brainpower. Minions followed orders without thinking for themselves.

Ellie smiled to herself. She could do this. Off she flew to find the real brains behind the badness.

CHAPTER 8

Archenemy Army

Ellie tried her luck in the main office. Maybe Dex was still on the phone with the pizza restaurant, giving the delivery address of his lair.

But when she looked inside, there was no Dex. The only sign of him was some marinara sauce fingerprints on the keypad. A little robot — no taller than Dex's knee — was dutifully cleaning them off.

Down the hall, a bot wheeled a cart of books into the library. The library! Dex could usually be found there reading *P.I. Pig*. It was all about a pig detective that solved cases around Farmtown. Ellie really wanted to read it, but Dex was being a major comic-book hog.

Ellie hid behind a bookshelf. From there she could see bots carting books up and down the aisles. They were stocking the shelves with Dex's favorites. There was *How to Rule the World (in Three Easy Steps), 101 Dirty Deeds for Minions,* and of course, *Super Blooper and Other No-Good Names for Superheroes.*

Ellie scanned the titles. Her eyes narrowed when she reached the end of the aisle. In the comic book section, *P.I. Pig* was blocked off by a red velvet rope. A Dex-bot was standing in front of it.

"Look with your eyes, not with your hands," it chanted.

"Ugh, I'll never get to read the comic now," Ellie muttered. "Not unless I use X-ray vision."

She slipped out and spotted more of Dex's handiwork around school. There was dried gum on drinking fountains, gummy worm sandwiches on the cafeteria menu, and a drawing of her with moose antlers. But she couldn't find the villain responsible.

Feeling frustrated, Ellie sat down on the stage in the auditorium. A banner hanging overhead read *Home of Dexter Archibald Diggs, Your Leader (Duh!).*

Out of nowhere, a group of Dex-bots appeared in the back of the room. "Superhero alert!" they shouted.

Two-by-two, they filed down the center aisle, their eyebeams focused on Ellie. The bots got ready to launch their pineapple projectiles.

"Oh, no you don't!" Ellie shouted. She jumped off the stage and charged the bots. Then she rolled herself into a spinning pink ball.

Ba-bam! Ba-bam! Ba-bam! Ellie plowed through Dex's minions with blurring speed. They flew this way and that, toppling like bowling pins. Strike!

Ellie skidded to a stop. Before the troops could get to their feet, she hurried out of the auditorium and flew to her locker. There, she unfastened her cape.

"This is making me a target," Ellie said, eyeing the shiny cloth. She grabbed her backpack out of her locker and stuffed her cape inside. It was OK to wear her cape at the REAL Winkopolis Elementary School. The leader of that school liked having a superhero around.

Vrooom! Just then Dex's monster trucks came from around the corner. As they raced toward Ellie, she escaped into the gym and shut the door firmly. But before she could breathe a sigh of relief, evil laughter echoed behind her.

"*Bwwa-ha-ha-HA!*" It was the laughter of mad scientists, wicked wizards, and third-grade troublemakers.

"Well, well, well," said Dex. "If it isn't Super Blooper!"

Ellie turned and saw Dex perched on an inflatable throne. The words *Bounce X-Treme* were written across the top. A Dex-bot stood nearby, holding a pizza box while Dex lounged lazily behind a big-screen TV. He had a video game remote control in one hand and an extra-cheesy slice of pizza in the other.

The Ultra Genie sat beside him.

"Dex! Give that back!" Ellie shouted, pointing at the genie. "You can't use a good gadget to do bad stuff. It's against the law of good!"

Dex took a huge bite out of his slice. "*Thish ish mwy shmool.*" He swallowed and started again. "This is my school. I can do whatever I want. I can have suckers at snack time and run rubber duck relay races in gym. I can even dress up like a badger for Spirit Day — and smell like one too!"

Eww, Ellie thought, scrunching her nose. The only thing worse than a villain was a *stinky* villain. "But you already got what you wanted. It's time to stop this!"

"Not a chance!" Dex grabbed the Ultra Genie and hopped down from his seat. "Ruling a school is fun. But I've been thinking . . . why should I stop here when I could rule the whole city? Now that would be *way* funner."

Dex snapped his fingers at the Dex-bot. The robot immediately made its way to the curtain behind Dex's throne. It tugged and tugged on a long rope. Slowly, the curtain parted, revealing a giant rotten pineapple face. It was made of metal, with a doorway that was shaped like a frown.

Dex swung an arm over the massive machine. "Meet my Dex-Bot Builder," he told Ellie. "I wished for one to make my own army of robots. Know what I'm gonna do with them? I'm gonna . . ."

"Take over Winkopolis?" Ellie guessed. She didn't have to read the villain's mind to figure out his plan.

"No interrupting!" Dex snapped. "But that's right. Take over Winkopolis. And when we're done, the city will be *ALL MINE!*" He reached for the control panel and pressed the ON button.

The Dex-Bot Builder roared to life. Its engine sputtered noisily as lights flashed and dials spun. A low rumble came from deep inside the machine and then — *Hic!*

The machine launched a Dex-bot out of its doorway. The bot marched to the front of Dex's throne and stood at attention.

Hic! Hic! The Dex-Bot Builder hiccupped again and again, launching more and more minions from its mouth. Five. Ten. Fifteen. Twenty. Line after line of them joined the ranks. They all stood attentively before their leader.

Ellie watched in horror as the gym filled with robo-archenemies. She ran to the machine and tried to press the OFF button, but it wouldn't budge.

"What's wrong with this thing?" she muttered. She flexed her muscle power and pushed with all of her might. But she couldn't turn off the Dex-Bot Builder.

A sly smile spread across Dex's face. "You can't stop it," he said. "Didn't I tell you? I wished for a machine that's superhero proof."

CHAPTER 9

Take Over

When the last bot marched into line, Dex turned off the Dex-Bot Builder with a tap of his finger. "Finally, I have enough bots to rule Winkopolis! Or better yet, *Dex Diggs City!*"

For a moment, Ellie imagined the streets swarming with minions and mini monster trucks. It wasn't good.

"Dex, I know you want to be a leader," she told him. "But you can do that without taking over towns and countries and planets. Why not start a club at school? Maybe you can make one for evil masterminds!"

Dex rubbed his chin thoughtfully. "That does sound cool. We could plot how to get free homework passes." Then he shook his head. "Naaah."

He strutted past his army, then climbed into his throne and stood on the seat. "Attention, minions!" he shouted at a sea of frowning faces. "I'm Dex Diggs, the boss around here. That means I give orders, and you follow them. If I tell you to wiggle your ears, you wiggle your ears. If I tell you to pat your bellies, you pat your bellies. If I tell you to sing 'Deck the Halls' — like a pirate — I better hear *Fa La La Matey* or you'll walk the plank! Got it?"

The Dex-bots' eyes flashed attentively.

"I have an order for you now, in fact," Dex continued. "I want to rule the city. That includes the parks, the pools, the arcades, and especially the ice cream store. They have the best sundaes ever. Did you tin heads hear me? You have to overthrow everything. And no matter what, don't stop until you *TAKE OVER!*"

"Take over! Take over!" the bots repeated. They marched off in all directions, following their leader's order exactly.

Some of the bots tore into Dex's pizza boxes and crammed cheesy slices into their mouths. Others picked up Dex's video game controllers. After loading a game called *Robot Dance Party*, they began to boogie down in front of the big-screen TV.

One bot broke away from the pack. "Take over! Take over!" it chanted, heading for the Dex-Bot Builder. Reaching the control panel, it pressed the *ON* button. Instantly, the Dex-Bot Builder fired up

again. It started churning out more minions with a
Hic! Hic! Hic!

Dex cried out at the minion mayhem. "Wait! No!
Don't touch that!" he shouted frantically.

But it was useless. The robots were on a mission
to take over — no matter what. They smashed Dex's
monster trucks together. They drew a goofy mustache
on his yearbook photo, which was framed on a wall
in twinkling lights.

Ellie shook her head at the master meanie's
meltdown. Sometimes, villains were just like cranky
toddlers. When they didn't get their way, they threw
tantrums!

Just then two bots snuck up behind the inflatable
throne. They took hold of the air plug and yanked
it open.

PFFFFT! Air rushed out with incredible force,
sending the throne — and Dex — up, up, and away.

"AAIYEE!" Dex shrieked while the giant chair flew skyward. He zipped and zoomed around the gym, holding on for dear life.

"Dex! I'll save you!" Ellie shouted. Fast as lightning, she bolted after him and grabbed his collar. She landed safely in the corner with Dex. The throne deflated as it flew past them and fell into a rumpled heap on the floor.

"My Dex-bots have gone bonkers!" Dex cried. "They should be invading Winkopolis right now. And getting me a Berry Blast Sundae!"

"They're following your orders," Ellie explained to him. "You *told* them to take over everything. And you told them not to stop — no matter what. They're going to keep this up even if you tell them not to."

Ellie thought for a moment. "Oh! I've got it! Why don't you make them self-destruct?" Usually, evil masterminds kept a self-destruct button for just such an emergency.

Dex only offered a blank stare.

"No self-destruct button? OK. Then we need the Ultra Genie . . ." Ellie hoped Dex would have the gadget, but his hands were empty. He must have lost it somewhere along the topsy-turvy throne ride!

Ellie glanced around the room. After a moment, the genie's coppery glow caught her super sight. It was lying next to the gym closet. Nearby, bots were building an enormous Dex-bot statue out of orange cones.

Noticing the gadget, one of the minions set down its cone. It picked up the genie, peeked inside, and began shaking it curiously. "Take over! Take over!" it chanted.

More bots joined their friend. One of them grabbed the genie's handle while a second grabbed the spout. They began to pull at both ends, trying to take the invention away from each other.

"They're going to pull apart Mom and Dad's invention!" Ellie cried.

If the Dex-bots broke the Ultra Genie, there would be no way to make Winkopolis Elementary School normal again. Everyone would be stuck in this no-good world. Forever!

CHAPTER 10

Dex the Superhero

Ellie sprang into action. She did not want to live in a world with hundreds of Dex look-a-likes. Having one archenemy was enough!

"Look out, robots! I'm coming for the Ultra Genie!" Ellie shouted. She spun herself into a whirling windstorm and twirled full-speed ahead.

Zing! Zing! Bots flew left and right as Ellie plowed into the mechanical crowd. She tried to push her way through, but more robots stepped in front of her. They marched out of the Dex-Bot Builder and blocked her from getting closer to the gadget. She tried a second time, then a third, then a fourth, whipping around with hurricane-like force to clear her path.

It was no use. As soon as the rush of wind tossed Dex's minions aside, new bots appeared. They would not let Ellie get anywhere near the genie.

"Whew, I'm dizzy!" Ellie said, finally rotating to a stop.

Dex ran up to her in a panic. "Why are you just standing here? Stop the bots!" he cried. "They're playing floor hockey with my monster trucks. And they're beating my score in *Robot Dance Party*!"

"I'm thinking of a plan B — B for *better*," Ellie replied.

If only Ellie could trick the robots into giving up the Ultra Genie. But how? She would need something else for them to go after, something like . . . a superhero.

"Wait a super second! That's it!" Ellie exclaimed. She unzipped her backpack and pulled out her cape. Then she handed it to Dex. "Here, put this on."

"Put *that* on?" Dex's face puckered at the sight of the shiny pink cloth. He looked like he had tried Dad's lemonade formula with extra sour power. "Not on your life! The bots will think I'm a superhero. I'll get pummeled with pineapples!"

"It's the only way to stop your army," Ellie argued. "Besides, if you wear the cape, you'll have the chance to save the city. Even the world . . ."

Dex crossed his arms.

"And maybe you'll get to rule another day," Ellie added. "I heard the Save the Slugs Club at school needs a captain."

"Gimme that." Dex grabbed Ellie's cape out of her hands. With a final grumble, he tied the fabric around his shoulders.

Ellie turned to the bots. "Oohh, Dex-bots! Look what I found!" she sang. "It's a do-gooding, cape-wearing . . . SUPERHERO!" She stepped aside and pointed at Dex.

The Dex-bots froze. Down went their hockey sticks, monster trucks, and video game controllers. Their eyebeams shot out and hit Ellie's cape in a flash.

"Superhero alert! Superhero alert!" the bots chanted. They began marching into an orderly line. It stretched the entire length of the gym, growing bot-by-bot with the help of the Dex-Bot Builder.

Dex's eyes widened, and he started shaking in his sneakers. "I'm going to be mush meat!" he cried, turning to Ellie. "What should I do?"

Ellie took a big breath and shouted, "RUN!"

"AAAHHH!" With a high-pitched howl, Dex took off across the gym. He passed the deflated throne and a pile of empty pizza boxes before shoving his way through the doors. Ellie's cape flapped behind him.

A flood of Dex-bots rushed after him. They ran past Ellie and poured into the hallway like a raging river.

Once the coast was clear, Ellie flew over and picked up the Ultra Genie. She frowned at the invention. It had helped her win votes. But it had also caused a lot of trouble.

There was a better way to prove she would make the best class president, Ellie realized. Even better than granting wishes for her classmates.

Rubbing the gadget, she said, "I wish I had never used the Ultra Genie."

Poof! A thin, milky cloud swirled out of the genie. It crept along the floor and crawled up the walls, covering every inch of the evil mastermind's lair until . . .

Dex Diggs Elementary School disappeared.

For good.

CHAPTER 11

A Super President

"Happy Election Day!"

Ellie blinked and found herself outside Miss Little's classroom. There, her teacher was greeting students as they arrived for school.

Miss Little waved a handful of ballots at Ellie. "Our class is all ready to vote this afternoon. Good luck in the election!"

"Election? That means . . ."

Ellie flew through the third-grade hallway. Reaching the end, she peered through the window. Beyond Miss Little's car in the parking lot, the school sign read *Winkopolis Elementary School.*

Ellie gasped. "My old school is back!" She caught a flash of pink in her reflection and smiled. "And so is my cape!"

"Drat, drat, drat . . ." At her locker, Payton was muttering as she kicked a flattened soccer ball. It was her lucky ball — the same one Ellie had magically fixed with the Ultra Genie.

Ellie floated over. "I thought your ball was fixed —"

Suddenly she stopped, remembering her last wish on the genie. All the wishes she'd granted with the Ultra Genie — Payton's ball, Joshua's skateboard, unlimited tacos at lunch, the fruit-juice fountain — had gone up in smoke with her last wish.

"What?" Payton made a confused face. "I wish it were fixed. I'll need all the luck I can get for my game tomorrow. We're playing a tough team — the Flying Scooters!"

As Payton started to put the ball away, a thought struck Ellie. She didn't have the Ultra Genie anymore, but she could still help — just like a good leader would.

"Be back in a second!" Ellie said. She zipped away, flying through the corridor and down the stairs.

She returned with tape and a pump from the gym equipment closet. After patching the hole made by Payton's soccer spikes, she flexed her muscle power and pumped up the ball until it was as good as new.

Payton happily bounced the ball on her knee. "You saved me! I can't wait to face those Flying Scooters now!"

"Flying . . . scooters?" a voice asked between breaths. "Can I have one?"

Ellie turned and saw Joshua. He was dragging his backpack, huffing and puffing like he had just outrun a mutant jellyfish.

"The bus missed my stop, so I had to walk the whole way here," he said. "I wish my skateboard weren't broken."

"Tell you what," Ellie said, scooping up his backpack. "I can fly you to school, at least until you get a new skateboard. How about it?"

"That'd be great!" Joshua replied.

Ellie carried his backpack to his locker for him. When the bell rang, they both hurried to class.

Dex surprised Ellie at the door. "Your do-gooding days are over," he said. "Today I'm getting elected. Prepare to meet your doom."

Ellie sighed. Dex didn't rule anymore, but clearly he was still the school's top troublemaker.

"We both have a chance to be class president," Ellie told him. "And when it's time to vote, may the best leader win!"

* * *

Ellie spent the rest of the morning doing super stuff — without the Ultra Genie. After announcements, she volunteered to empty the recycling bin. Then she helped Amanda finish a poem in language arts.

"What word rhymes with *flower*?" Amanda asked, tapping her notebook with a pencil.

"Well, there's *hour, shower, sour, tower . . .*" Ellie rattled off rhyming words that flashed like fireworks in her mind. "And then there's *power,* as in Princess Power — the greatest comic book superhero in the universe!"

At recess, she worked with Hannah on her audition for *Dancing Snowflake.* She watched as Hannah twirled around the field like a real snowflake.

Hannah took a bow when her routine was over. "How was that?" she asked Ellie eagerly.

"It was awesome!" Ellie replied. "You're a shoe-in for the lead role. Still, I'll keep my fingers crossed for you!"

When math rolled around later, Ellie offered to give Owen a hand with his worksheet. But he was already done, thanks to her earlier advice.

"I remembered what you told me, so it was easy," Owen said. He swung his fist in the air. "POW! Take that, two-digit multiplication!"

Owen ran off to hand in the assignment. He hurried past Dex, who was putting the finishing touches on a dried gum sculpture.

Ellie snuck a peek at his chewed-up masterpiece. She shuddered. It looked like a mini model of the Dex-Bot Builder.

Finally, social studies arrived. Miss Little stood in front of the class.

"Before you voice your presidential choice, each candidate will make a final statement," the teacher said. She turned to Dex. "Let's hear your statement first, Candidate Diggs."

Dex blabbed on about his phony promises. He ended with, "And furthermore, when Miss Little puts me in charge, I will treat my minions — er, I mean, *classmates* — fairly. Everyone will get a turn on the twisty slide. But remember . . ." He poked the sky with his finger. "I go first."

"Thank you, Dex," Miss Little said. She looked at the clock. "Ellie? Let's hear from you. I think we have just enough time."

"Enough time for you to *give up*," Dex teased as Ellie passed him in the aisle.

Taking the floor, Ellie smiled at her fellow class citizens. She liked granting wishes for them. But she didn't have the power to do that anymore. She would have to prove why she would make the best president the only way she could.

"Dex has made a lot of promises," Ellie began. "But the truth is, I can only make one promise. I will always try to be a good leader. I will continue to be honest and helpful. And I will work with everyone — no matter if I win or lose." Her hand went up. "Superhero's honor."

The class clapped as Ellie sat down quietly. "Voting time!" Miss Little announced, handing out ballots.

Soon pencils scribbled away, selecting the lucky candidate who would soon lead Room #128. Then Miss Little came around with the official ballot box. Dex dropped in his ballot and sat back confidently.

Ellie watched as everyone handed in his or her ballot. She hoped her good deeds had been good enough to get her elected. Still, if Dex came out ahead, would it be so bad? Sure, he would probably stick her with classroom cleanup duty. But at least she wouldn't have to deal with pesky robots on the playground.

Moments later, the votes were tallied. "And our class president is . . ."

Ellie fidgeted in her seat. Dex turned to Ellie and put on a huge smile.

Miss Little's head popped up from her desk. "Ellie! Ellie is our new class president!"

As applause filled the room, Dex lost his balance and fell out of his chair. "What? I demand a recount," he said, scrambling to his feet. "It's a mistake — a *mistake*, I tell you! My plan was superhero proof!"

"I'm class president? I'm class president!" Ellie beamed brightly. Her class had picked her! She felt like she had fought an epic battle between good and evil — and won.

Hannah patted Ellie on the shoulder. "I knew you'd win. It doesn't take X-ray vision to see through Dex's promises." She giggled. "Thanks for helping me practice for my audition."

"And thanks for fixing my ball," Payton added from the next row. "See you at my game tomorrow?"

"I'll be there!" Ellie said.

Just then, a soft whimper came from the corner. Ellie turned to see Dex, who was not taking his

defeat well. He was pouting in the worst way, his bottom lip sticking out far enough for a little bird to perch on it.

Poor Dex, Ellie thought. *He really did want to win badly.*

It was time to do something good — for Dex.

"You know, running a whole class is a lot of work," Ellie said to him. "I'll probably need a hand. Since you like taking charge of stuff, do you want to help?"

Dex's face, which was as wrinkled as a raisin, slowly smoothed. "Really?" he asked.

"Sure," she replied. "Just promise me one thing. No Dex-bots. OK?"

Dex looked confused, but he nodded anyway.

As class president, Ellie had done her first good deed. And she didn't even need the power of the genie to do it. Being kind. Cooperative. Honest. Helpful. It was what being a good leader — even a *super* one — was all about.

GLOSSARY

about-face (uh-BOWT FAYS) — to turn completely around

android (AN-droyd) — a human-like robot

archenemy (ARCH EN-uh-me) — a person's main enemy

betterment (BET-uhr-mehnt) — making something better

domination (dahm-uh-NAY-shun) — to rule over someone or something completely

marinara (mare-uh-NARE-uh) — a sauce made with tomatoes

mayhem (MAY-hehm) — chaos and destruction

minions (MIN-yuhns) — people or things that follow a leader and do things without question

podium (POH-dee-uhm) — a high, small table people often stand behind when speaking in front of crowds

recount (REE-cownt) — the process of counting ballots or votes again

scowl (SKOWL) — to look angry and frown

stink eye (stingk ahy) — giving someone a dirty look

TALK ABOUT ELLIE!

1. A good leader has many qualities, including being cooperative, fair, and helpful. Talk about the qualities that make a good leader. Why are they important for a leader to have?

2. Ellie grants wishes for her classmates to win their votes. Do you think it was right of her to use the Ultra Genie? Why or why not?

3. Dex thinks he will win the election by making promises he can't keep. Talk about some of the promises he makes, then talk about why candidates should do their best to keep their promises.

EXPRESS YOURSELF!

1. Imagine you are running for class president. Create a campaign poster — like Ellie and her friends do in this story — to convince people to vote for you.

2. In her speech, Ellie promises to listen to others and try to fix her mistakes. She'll even fight mutant pigeons! Imagine you are a candidate like Ellie. Write a speech that explains what you would do as a leader.

3. In the beginning of the story, Ellie's class gives examples of good leaders in history — presidents like George Washington and Abraham Lincoln. Flex your brainpower and do research on one of the presidents. Then write a paragraph about why that president was a good leader.

ABOUT THE AUTHOR

Gina Bellisario is an ordinary grown-up who can do many extraordinary things. She can make things disappear, such as a cheeseburger or a grass stain. She can create a masterpiece out of glitter glue and shoelaces. She can even thwart a messy room with her super cleaning power! Gina lives in Park Ridge, Illinois, not too far from Winkopolis, with her husband and their super kids.

ABOUT THE ILLUSTRATOR

Jessika von Innerebner loves creating — especially when it inspires and empowers others to make the world a better place. She landed her first illustration job at the age of seventeen and hasn't looked back since. Jess is an illustrator who loves humor and heart and has colored her way through projects with Disney.com, Nickelodeon, Fisher-Price, and Atomic Cartoons, to name a few. In her spare moments, Jess can be found long-boarding, yoga-ing, dancing, adventuring to distant lands, and laughing with friends. She currently lives in sunny Kelowna, Canada.

CHECK OUT THE REST OF ELLIE'S EXTRAORDINARY ADVENTURES!

Superhero for President

by Gina Bellisario
illustrated by Jessika von Innerebner

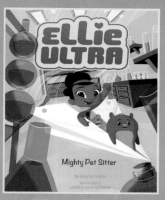

Mighty Pet Sitter

by Gina Bellisario
illustrated by Jessika von Innerebner

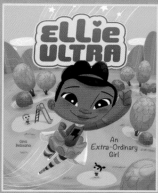

An Extra-Ordinary Girl

Gina Bellisario

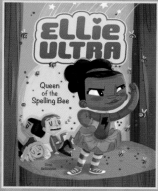

Queen of the Spelling Bee

Gina Bellisario

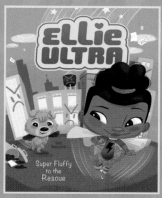

Super Fluffy to the Rescue

Gina Bellisario

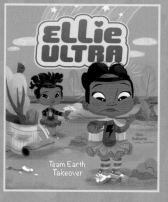

Team Earth Takeover

Gina Bellisario

ONLY FROM CAPSTONE!

THE FUN DOESN'T STOP HERE!

Discover more at *www.capstonekids.com*

Videos and Contests
Games and Puzzles
Friends and Favorites
Authors and Illustrators

Find cool websites and more books like this one
at *www.facthound.com.* Just type in the
Book ID: 9781496552396 and you're ready to go!